NICK JR.
DORA the EXPLORER

Pack 1

PHONIC
READING PRO

10652636

Let's Explore!

**Explore With Dora · Isa's Little Fish · Dora's Lost List
Stuck in the Mud! · Friends Out West! · Hope You Can Come!**

SCHOLASTIC INC.

New York   Toronto   London   Auckland   Sydney
Mexico City   New Delhi   Hong Kong   Buenos Aires

No part of this publication may be reproduced in whole or in part, stored in a
retrieval system, or transmitted in any form or by any means, electronic, mechanical,
photocopying, recording, or otherwise, without written permission of the publisher.
For information regarding permission, write to Scholastic Inc.,
Attention: Permissions Department, 557 Broadway, New York, NY 10012.

Dora the Explorer™: Explore With Dora (0-439-67755-6) © 2004 Viacom International Inc.
Dora the Explorer™: Isa's Little Fish (0-439-67756-4) © 2004 Viacom International Inc.
Dora the Explorer™: Dora's Lost List (0-439-67757-2) © 2004 Viacom International Inc.
Dora the Explorer™: Stuck in the Mud! (0-439-67758-0) © 2004 Viacom International Inc.
Dora the Explorer™: Friends Out West! (0-439-67759-9) © 2004 Viacom International Inc.
Dora the Explorer™: Hope You Can Come! (0-439-67760-2) © 2004 Viacom International Inc.

NICKELODEON, NICK JR., Dora the Explorer, and all related titles, logos, and characters are
trademarks of Viacom International Inc. All rights reserved.

Used under license by Scholastic Inc. Published by Scholastic Inc. SCHOLASTIC
and associated logos are trademarks and/or registered trademarks of Scholastic Inc.

ISBN-13: 978-0-439-90237-3
ISBN-10: 0-439-90237-1

12 11 10 9 8 7 6 5 4 3 2 1   6 7 8 9 10 11/0

Printed in the U.S.A.
This compilation edition first printing, September 2006

PHONICS
READING PROGRAM

Welcome to **Dora the Explorer's** Phonics Reading Program!

Learning to read is so important for your child's success in school and in life. Now **Dora the Explorer** is here to help your child learn important phonics skills. Here's how the following six stories work:

Take phonics, the fundamental skill of knowing that the letters we read represent the sounds we hear and say. Add **Dora** and help your child LEARN to read and LOVE to read!

To be a good reader, it takes practice. That's where **Dora the Explorer** can make a difference. Kids love **Dora** and will want to read her latest adventures over and over again. Try these ideas for enjoying the books with your child:

- Read together by taking turns line by line or page by page.

- Look for all the words that have the sound being featured in the reader. Read them over and over again.

- Have your child read the story to you and then retell it in his or her own words.

Scholastic has been helping families encourage young readers for more than 80 years. Thank you for letting us help you support your beginning reader.

Happy reading,

Francie Alexander,
Chief Academic Officer, Scholastic Inc.

In this story, you can learn all about the short "a" sound. Here are some words to sound out.

bag   **jam**

flap   **map**

glad   **pal**

These are words that you will see in this story and many other stories. You will want to learn them as well.

can   **no**   **is**   **it**   **know**

These are some more challenging words that you will see in this story.

adventure   **explore**   **friends**

animal   **family**   **spacecraft**

NICK JR.

DORA the EXPLORER

PHONICS
READING PROGRAM

Book 1
short a

Explore With Dora

by Quinlan B. Lee

SCHOLASTIC INC.

New York   Toronto   London   Auckland   Sydney
Mexico City   New Delhi   Hong Kong   Buenos Aires

Hi!
I am Dora.
I am glad that
you are here.

I like to go
on adventures.
I can go by raft
or blast off
in a spacecraft.

After an adventure,
I always go home
to my family.
We live in a warm land
with lots of animal friends.

This is my best pal, Boots.
Do you know
his favorite snack?
Is it apples?
Ham?
Jam?
No!
It is bananas.

We love to explore.
Whom do we ask
where to go?
He is flat
and knows the path.
A plan?
A pad?
No!
It is Map!
Map keeps us on track.

How can I carry Map?
Do I have a sack?
A bag?
A basket?
No!
I have Backpack.
She has two straps
and a flap.

I am happy you came.

In this story, you can learn all about the short "i" sound. Here are some words to sound out.

fit   **fish**

hill   **swim**

in   **this**

These are words that you will see in this story and many other stories. You will want to learn them as well.

back   **his**   **little**   **way**   **will**

These are some more challenging words that you will see in this story.

bridge   **iguana**   **riddle**

hidden   **tricky**   **spring**

NICK JR.

DORA the EXPLORER

PHONICS
READING PROGRAM

Book 2
short i

Isa's Little Fish

by Quinlan B. Lee

SCHOLASTIC INC.

New York   Toronto   London   Auckland   Sydney
Mexico City   New Delhi   Hong Kong   Buenos Aires

Oh, no!
That is Swiper!
If he has a plan to swipe,
say "Swiper, no swiping!"
as fast as you can.
Say it three times
and he will scram!
Oh, man!

This is our friend Isa.
She is an iguana.
She found a little fish.

Little Fish is lost.
He misses his family.
Will you help him
swim back home?
How will we know
where he lives?

Right!
Ask Map.
Map says that
Little Fish should swim
under the bridge,
in between the big rocks,
and into the spring.
We will walk next to you,
Little Fish!

Oh, no!
This is the Grumpy
Old Troll's bridge.
We have to answer
his tricky riddle.
Ready?
In this school
you learn to swim,
gills are cool,
and fins are in.
What is it?
It is a school of fish.
Yeah!

Now, which way
should Little Fish swim?
Great!
He needs to slip in
between the big rocks.
Will he fit?

He did!
I see the spring.
It is hidden
behind that hill.
Swim, Little Fish!
Swim!

We did it!
Little Fish is back
in the spring.

What a trip!

In this story, you can learn all about the short "o" sound. Here are some words to sound out.

got   **pops**

hot   **shop**

lost   **top**

These are words that you will see in this story and many other stories. You will want to learn them as well.

have   **I**   **look**   **not**   **to**

These are some more challenging words that you will see in this story.

bread   **hollow**   **pocket**

crossed   **maybe**   **raisins**

NICK JR

PHONICS
READING PROGRAM

Dora's Lost List

by Quinlan B. Lee

SCHOLASTIC INC.

New York   Toronto   London   Auckland   Sydney
Mexico City   New Delhi   Hong Kong   Buenos Aires

ice pops

box of raisins

hot, soft bread

My mom gave us
a shopping list.
It says to buy
ice pops,
a box of raisins,
and hot, soft bread.
Let's go shop!

We are almost at the
shop.
But where is our list?
Oh, no!
It is lost!
I know it said to buy
a box of raisins
and hot, soft bread.
What did it say on top?
We have got to find it.

How will we find it?
Right!
Go back and check
all the spots
where we stopped.

I know we stopped
at a hollow log.
Look!
Do you see the log?
Maybe the list
is lost inside it.

It is not in the log.
Before the log,
we saw a frog hop.
Where did we spot the frog?
We were by the frog pond.
Come on!

No list.
Let's go ask Mom
for a new list.
First we have to
cross the pond.
Let's go across
on the rocks.

Stop! I've got it!
Last time we
crossed the rocks,
Boots did not want
to drop the list.
Where did he put it?
In his pocket!
Yeah!
We got the lost list.

ice pops

box of raisins

hot, soft bread

Look, it said ice pops. Mmmm.

In this story, you can learn all about the short
"u" sound. Here are some words to sound out.

bugs   **mud**

bunch   **stuck**

luck   **up**

These are words that you will see in this story
and many other stories. You will want to learn
them as well.

back   **in**   **must**   **out**

These are some more challenging words that
you will see in this story.

butterflies   **something**   **without**

jump   **enough**   **wonder**

NICK JR.

PHONICS
READING PROGRAM

Stuck in the Mud!

by Quinlan B. Lee

SCHOLASTIC INC.

New York   Toronto   London   Auckland   Sydney
Mexico City   New Delhi   Hong Kong   Buenos Aires

What a sunny day!
Boots and I love to run
and chase after butterflies.

Stop!
Do you see something
under that bush?
It is a Bugga Bugga baby.
But what is she doing
under those shrubs?

Uh-oh!
The little bug is stuck
in the mud.
Come on!
We must pull her out
and get her back home.

There's so much mud!
How can we get her
unstuck without getting
stuck in the muck, too?
Right!
Jump on the rocks.

Good jumping!
Now we're close enough.
Come on,
Baby Bugga Bugga.
We will help you up
and out of the mud.

We did it!
But now we must
take her home.
I wonder where
Bugga Bugga bugs live.

Bugga Bugga bugs
love flowers.
With some luck,
we can find her momma
in this bunch of flowers.

Yay! The baby bug
is back with her mother.

In this story, you can learn all about the short "e" sound. Here are some words to sound out.

bed **then**

fed **vest**

red **went**

These are words that you will see in this story and many other stories. You will want to learn them as well.

get **go** **the** **through**

These are some more challenging words that you will see in this story.

desert **happy** **straight**

echo **horses** **tunnel**

NICK JR

DORA the EXPLORER

PHONICS
READING PROGRAM

Book 5
short e

Friends Out West!

by Quinlan B. Lee

SCHOLASTIC INC.

New York   Toronto   London   Auckland   Sydney
Mexico City   New Delhi   Hong Kong   Buenos Aires

Howdy, explorers!
I am Cowgirl Dora,
dressed in
my best vest
and boots.
Will you help me in my
wild west adventure?

My friend, Cowboy Boots,
and I went for a long ride.
We are ready
to head home.
First, we must
get our horses
back to Benny's barn
to be fed.
How do we get there?

Check Map!
Map says,
"Go into Echo Tunnel.
Then head through
the desert rocks,
and straight ahead
to Benny's barn."
Ready?
Let's go!

Here is a tunnel.
Is it Echo Tunnel?
How can we check?
Right!
Make an echo.
Will you help me?

Let's yell "hello!"
The tunnel said
"hello" back.
Is that an echo?
Yes!
It is Echo Tunnel.

Where did Map
tell us to go next?
Right!
Head through
the desert rocks.
Up ahead
I see something red.
Let's get going!

Benny's barn!
We made it to the end
of the trail.
Now we can get to bed.

So long, friends.
Happy trails!

In this story, you can learn all about the final "e" sounds. Here are some words to sound out.

bake	**here**
cake	**huge**
five	**notes**

These are words that you will see in this story and many other stories. You will want to learn them as well.

came   **come**   **we**   **you**

These are some more challenging words that you will see in this story.

games	**invite**	**slices**
great	**mistake**	**tastes**

NICK JR

DORA the EXPLORER

PHONICS
READING PROGRAM

Hope You Can Come!

by Quinlan B. Lee

SCHOLASTIC INC.

New York   Toronto   London   Auckland   Sydney
Mexico City   New Delhi   Hong Kong   Buenos Aires

We love to bake cakes!
We used all these things
on the table.
I hope it tastes great!

We made a huge cake!
Boots and I can't eat
the whole thing.
What can we do
with all the slices?

Let's have a party.
We can invite
five friends over
to share a slice
of cake with us.
We can make hats
and play games.
It will be a great time!
First, we'll write
their names on notes.

I hope all of our friends can come.
Let's take them their notes.

It is time for the party!
Is everyone here?
Count our friends.
One, two, three, four . . .
someone is late.
Did he hide outside?

Yes! It is Swiper!
Look at his face.
Don't worry, Swiper,
there is no mistake.
We gave you a note.

We are glad you came.
Come in.
Play a game.
Make a hat and
share some cake.